FOX IN SOCKS
AND OTHER STORIES

CONTENTS

Fox in Socks and Other Stories
™ & © Dr. Seuss Enterprises, L.P. 2003
All rights reserved

This omnibus edition first published 2003 by Carnival
an imprint of HarperCollins*Publishers* Ltd
77-85 Fulham Palace Road, London W6 8JB

The HarperCollins website address is:
www.harpercollins.co.uk

ISBN 0 00 774941 4

Fox in Socks © 1965 by
Dr. Seuss Enterprises, L.P. All rights reserved.
A Beginner Book published by arrangement with
Random House Inc., New York, USA
First published in the UK 1966
Mr Brown Can Moo! Can You? © 1970 by
Dr. Seuss Enterprises, L.P. All rights reserved.
A Bright and Early Book for Beginning Beginners
Published by arrangement with
Random House, Inc., New York, USA
First published in the UK 1971
Marvin K. Mooney Will You Please Go Now! © 1972 by
Dr. Seuss Enterprises, L.P. All rights reserved.
A Bright and Early Book for Beginning Beginners
Published by arrangement with
Random House Inc., New York, USA
First published in the UK 1973

Printed in China

Fox

Socks

Box

Knox

Knox in box.
Fox in socks.

Knox on fox
in socks in box.

Socks on Knox
and Knox in box.

Fox in socks
on box on Knox.

Chicks with bricks come.
Chicks with blocks come.
Chicks with bricks and
blocks and clocks come.

Look, sir. Look, sir.
Mr. Knox, sir.
Let's do tricks with
bricks and blocks, sir.
Let's do tricks with
chicks and clocks, sir.

First, I'll make a
quick trick brick stack.
Then I'll make a
quick trick block stack.

You can make a
quick trick chick stack.
You can make a
quick trick clock stack.

And here's a
new trick, Mr. Knox. . . .
Socks on chicks
and chicks on fox.
Fox on clocks
on bricks and blocks.
Bricks and blocks
on Knox on box.

Now we come to
ticks and tocks, sir.
Try to say this
Mr. Knox, sir. . . .

Clocks on fox tick.
Clocks on Knox tock.
Six sick bricks tick.
Six sick chicks tock.

Please, sir. I don't
like this trick, sir.
My tongue isn't
quick or slick, sir.
I get all those
ticks and clocks, sir,
mixed up with the
chicks and tocks, sir.
I can't do it, Mr. Fox, sir.

I'm so sorry,
Mr. Knox, sir.

Here's an easy
game to play.
Here's an easy
thing to say. . . .

New socks.
Two socks.
Whose socks?
Sue's socks.

Who sews whose socks?
Sue sews Sue's socks.

Who sees who sew
whose new socks, sir?
You see Sue sew
Sue's new socks, sir.

That's not easy,
Mr. Fox, sir.

Who comes? . . .
Crow comes.
Slow Joe Crow comes.

Who sews crow's clothes?
Sue sews crow's clothes.
Slow Joe Crow
sews whose clothes?
Sue's clothes.

Sue sews socks of
fox in socks now.

Slow Joe Crow sews
Knox in box now.

Sue sews rose
on Slow Joe Crow's clothes.
Fox sews hose
on Slow Joe Crow's nose.

Hose goes.
Rose grows.
Nose hose goes some.
Crow's rose grows some.

Mr. Fox!
I hate this game, sir.
This game makes
my tongue quite lame, sir.

Mr. Knox, sir,
what a shame, sir.

We'll find something
new to do now.
Here is lots of
new blue goo now.
New goo. Blue goo.
Gooey. Gooey.
Blue goo. New goo.
Gluey. Gluey.

Gooey goo
for chewy chewing!
That's what that
Goo-Goose is doing.
Do you choose to
chew goo, too, sir?
If, sir, you, sir,
choose to chew, sir,
with the Goo-Goose,
chew, sir. Do, sir.

Mr. Fox, sir,
I won't do it.
I can't say it.
I won't chew it.

Very well, sir.
Step this way.
We'll find another
game to play.

Bim comes.
Ben comes.
Bim brings Ben broom.
Ben brings Bim broom.

Ben bends Bim's broom.
Bim bends Ben's broom.
Bim's bends.
Ben's bends.
Ben's bent broom breaks.
Bim's bent broom breaks.

Ben's band. Bim's band.
Big bands. Pig bands.

Bim and Ben lead
bands with brooms.
Ben's band bangs
and Bim's band booms.

Pig band! Boom band!
Big band! Broom band!
My poor mouth can't
say that. No, sir.
My poor mouth is
much too slow, sir.

Well then . . .
bring your mouth this way.
I'll find it something
it can say.

Luke Luck likes lakes.
Luke's duck likes lakes.
Luke Luck licks lakes.
Luke's duck licks lakes.

Duck takes licks
in lakes Luke Luck likes.
Luke Luck takes licks
in lakes duck likes.

I can't blab
such blibber blubber!
My tongue isn't
made of rubber.

Mr. Knox. Now
come now. Come now.
You don't have to
be so dumb now. . . .

Try to say this,
Mr. Knox, please. . . .

Through three cheese trees
three free fleas flew.
While these fleas flew,
freezy breeze blew.
Freezy breeze made
these three trees freeze.
Freezy trees made
these trees' cheese freeze.
That's what made these
three free fleas sneeze.

Stop it! Stop it!
That's enough, sir.
I can't say
such silly stuff, sir.

Very well, then,
Mr. Knox, sir.

Let's have a little talk
about tweetle beetles. . . .

What do you know
about tweetle beetles?
Well . . .

When tweetle beetles fight,
it's called
a tweetle beetle battle.

And when they
battle in a puddle,
it's a tweetle
beetle puddle battle.

AND when tweetle beetles
battle with paddles in a puddle,
they call it a tweetle
beetle puddle paddle battle.
                    AND . . .

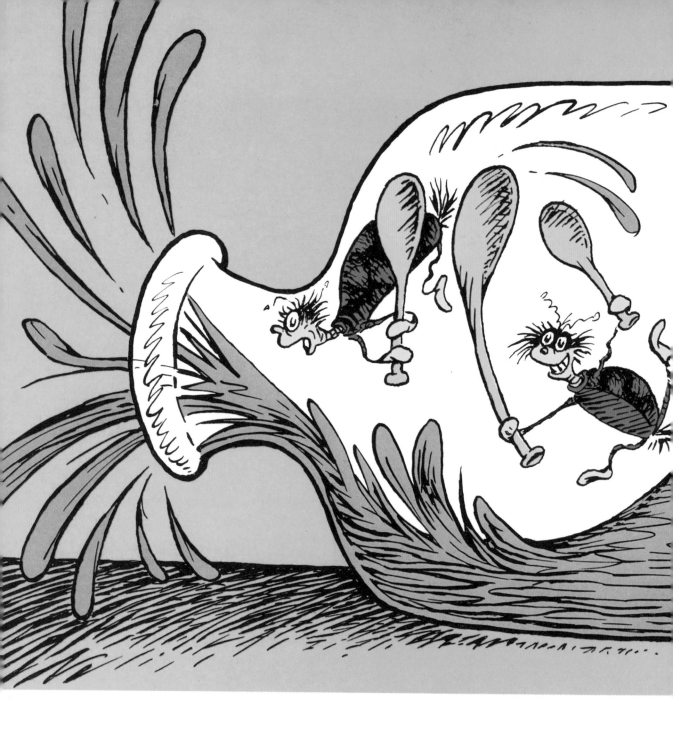

When beetles battle beetles
in a puddle paddle battle
and the beetle battle puddle
is a puddle in a bottle . . .

. . . they call this
a tweetle beetle
bottle puddle
paddle battle muddle.
AND . . .

When beetles
fight these battles
in a bottle
with their paddles
and the bottle's
on a poodle
and the poodle's
eating noodles . . .

. . . they call this
a muddle puddle
tweetle poodle
beetle noodle
bottle paddle battle.
AND . . .

Now wait
a minute,
Mr. Socks Fox!

When a fox is
in the bottle where
the tweetle beetles battle
with their paddles
in a puddle on a
noodle-eating poodle,
THIS is what they call . . .

. . . a tweetle beetle
noodle poodle bottled
paddled muddled duddled
fuddled wuddled
fox in socks, sir!

Fox in socks,
our game is done, sir.
Thank you for
a lot of fun, sir.

Mr. Brown Can MOO!

Can You?

By Dr. Seuss

Oh, the wonderful things
Mr. Brown can do!
He can go like a cow.
He can go MOO MOO
Mr. Brown can do it.
How about you?

He can go like a bee.

Mr. Brown can

BUZZ

How about you?
Can you go

BUZZ
BUZZ

He can go
like a cork . . .

POP POP

POP

POP

He can go like horse feet

He can go

EEK
EEK

like a squeaky shoe.

He can go
like a rooster . . .

COCK A
DOODLE
DOO

He can go
like an owl . . .

HOO HOO
HOO HOO

EEK EEK
EEK EEK
COCK-A-DOODLE-DOO
HOO HOO HOO HOO

How about you?

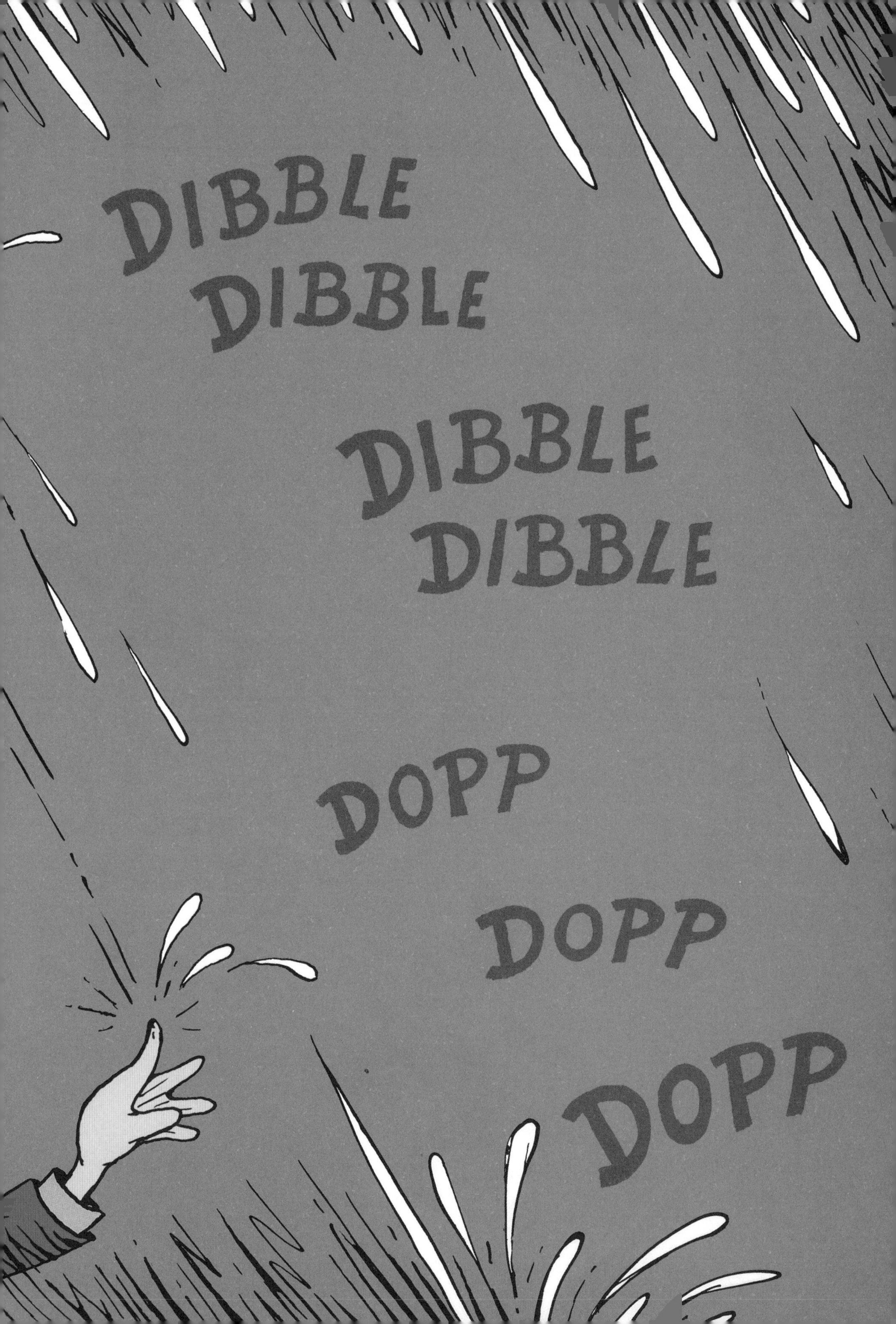
DIBBLE
DIBBLE
DIBBLE
DIBBLE
DOPP
DOPP
DOPP

He can go like a train

CHOO CHOO
CHOO
CHOO

Oh, the wonderful things
Mr. Brown can do!

Moo Moo
Buzz Buzz
Pop Pop Pop
Eek Eek
Hoo Hoo
Klopp Klopp Klopp
Dibble Dibble
Dopp Dopp
Cock-a-Doodle-Doo

Mr. Brown can do it.
How about you?

. . . like the soft,
soft whisper
of a butterfly.

Maybe YOU can, too.
I think you ought to try.

He can go
like a horn. . .

BLURP
BLURP
BLURP
BLURP

He can go like a clock.
He can

TICK

He can

TOCK

He can go
like a hand
on a door . . .

Oh, the wonderful things
Mr. Brown can do!

BLURP BLURP
SLURP SLURP

COCK-A-DOODLE-DOO

KNOCK KNOCK KNOCK

and HOO HOO HOO

He can even

SIZZLE
SIZZLE

He can do that, too,
like an egg
in a frying pan.
How about you?

Mr. Brown is smart,
as smart as they come!
He can do
a hippopotamus
chewing gum!

GRUM
GRUM

GRUM
GRUM

GRUM
GRUM
GRUM

Mr. Brown is
so smart
he can even do this:
he can even
make a noise
like a goldfish kiss!

BOOM BOOM BOOM

Mr. Brown is a wonder!

BOOM BOOM BOOM

Mr. Brown makes thunder!

He makes lightning!

SPLATT SPLATT SPLATT

And it's very, very hard
to make a noise like that.

Oh, the wonderful things
Mr. Brown can do!

Moo Moo
Buzz Buzz
Pop Pop Pop

    Eek Eek
    Hoo Hoo
    Klopp Klopp Klopp

Dibble Dibble
Dopp Dopp
Cock-a-Doodle-Doo

    Grum Grum
    Grum Grum
    Choo Choo Choo

Boom Boom
Splatt Splatt
Tick Tick Tock

    Sizzle Sizzle
    Blurp Blurp
    Knock Knock Knock

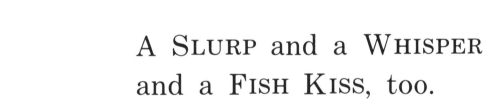

A Slurp and a Whisper
and a Fish Kiss, too.

Mr. Brown can do it.
How about YOU?

Marvin K. Mooney Will you

PLEASE

GO

NOW!

BY Dr. Seuss

The
time
has come.

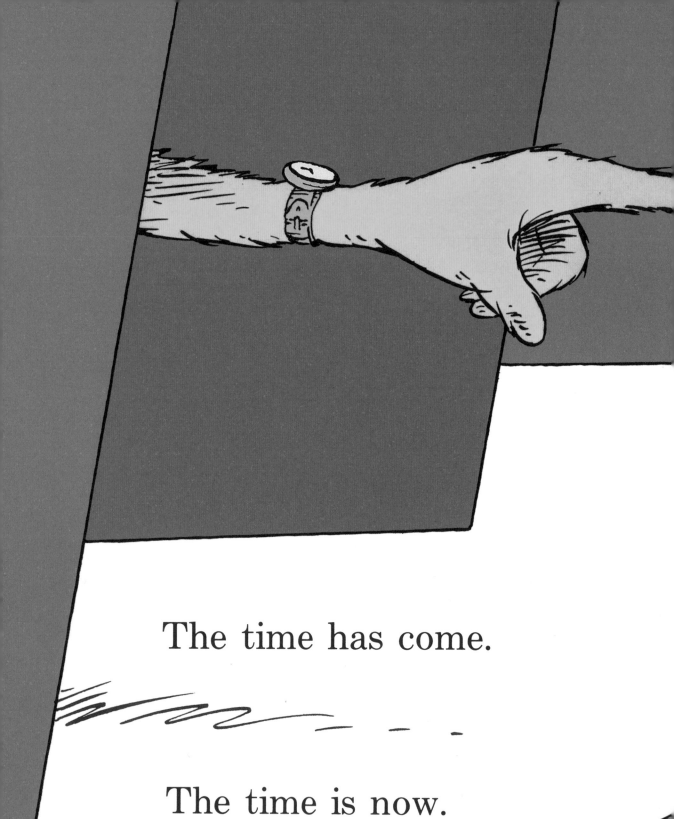

The time has come.

The time is now.

Just go.
Go.
GO!
I don't care how.

You can go by foot.

You can go
by cow.

Marvin K. Mooney,
will you
please go now!

You can go
on skates.

You can go
on skis.

You can go
in a hat.

But
please go.
Please!

If you like
you can go
in an old blue shoe.

Just go, go, GO!
Please do, do, DO!

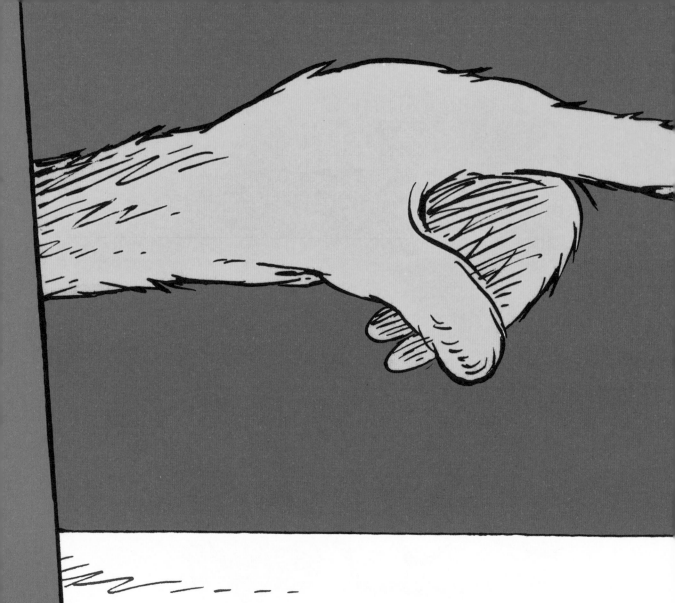

Marvin K. Mooney,
I don't care how.
Marvin K. Mooney,
will you please
GO NOW!

You can go on stilts.

You can go by fish.

You can go
in a Crunk-Car
if you wish.

If you wish
you may go
by lion's tail.

Or stamp yourself
and go by mail.

Marvin K. Mooney!
Don't you know
the time has come
to go, Go, GO!

Get on your way!
Please, Marvin K.!
You might like going
In a Zumble-Zay.

You can go
by balloon ...

... or broomstick.

OR

You can go
by camel
in a
bureau drawer.

You can go by Bumble-Boat . . .

. . . or jet.

I don't care
how you go.

Just GET!

Get yourself a Ga-Zoom.

You can go with a ......

Marvin, Marvin, Marvin!
Will you leave this room!

Marvin K. Mooney!
I don't care HOW.

Marvin K. Mooney!

Will you please

GO NOW!

I said

GO

and

GO

I meant....

The time had come.
SO . . .
Marvin WENT.